SECRETS OF AN OVERWORLD SURVIVOR
WOLVES VS. ZOMBIES

GREYSON MANN

ILLUSTRATED BY GRACE SANDFORD

Sky Pony Press
New York

Copyright © 2017 by Hollan Publishing, Inc.

Minecraft® is a registered trademark of Notch Development AB.

The Minecraft game is copyright © Mojang AB.

This book is not authorized or sponsored by Microsoft Corp., Mojang AB, Notch Development AB or Scholastic Inc., or any other person or entity owning or controlling rights in the Minecraft name, trademark, or copyrights.

All rights reserved. No part of this book may be reproduced in any manner without the express written consent of the publisher, except in the case of brief excerpts in critical reviews or articles. All inquiries should be addressed to Sky Pony Press, 307 West 36th Street, 11th Floor, New York, NY 10018.

Sky Pony Press books may be purchased in bulk at special discounts for sales promotion, corporate gifts, fund-raising, or educational purposes. Special editions can also be created to specifications. For details, contact the Special Sales Department, Sky Pony Press, 307 West 36th Street, 11th Floor, New York, NY 10018 or info@skyhorsepublishing.com.

Sky Pony® is a registered trademark of Skyhorse Publishing, Inc.®, a Delaware corporation.

Minecraft® is a registered trademark of Notch Development AB.
The Minecraft game is copyright © Mojang AB.

Visit our website at www.skyponypress.com.

10 9 8 7 6 5 4 3 2 1

Library of Congress Cataloging-in-Publication Data is available on file.
Special thanks to Erin L. Falligant.

Cover illustration by Grace Sandford
Cover design by Brian Peterson

Paperback ISBN: 978-1-5107-1333-8
Ebook ISBN: 978-1-5107-1332-1

Printed in Canada

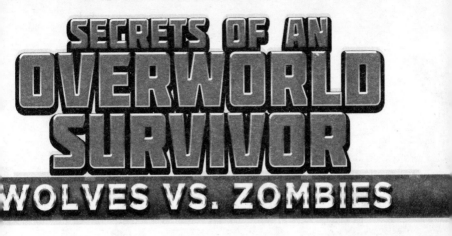

SECRETS OF AN OVERWORLD SURVIVOR

WOLVES VS. ZOMBIES

CHAPTER 1

Plink!

Something cold and wet pinged onto Will's forehead and dripped down his cheek. He glanced at the icy structure towering above him. *It must be twenty feet tall!* he guessed, shading his eyes to see the top.

Jagged ice sculptures littered the landscape. Traveling through them,

Will felt as if he were surrounded by an army of iron golems.

It was slow going—cold, wet, and slippery. But crossing the ice plains was the only way to get to the taiga biome. He gazed at the snowcapped mountain range ahead. He was so close now!

In just a few hours, he would wander through the spruce forest at the top of those hills. Throw snowballs. *And finally build a snow golem*, he thought with a happy shiver.

He looked back at his sled, where a flame-orange pumpkin rested in a nest of blankets. His brother, Seth, thought he was foolish for bringing that heavy pumpkin all the way from the farm.

But what's a snow golem without a pumpkin? thought Will. *Just a boring old snowman.* If he put a pumpkin on its head, the snowman would come to life as a snow golem—at least, that's what he'd heard.

Will grinned at the thought. Then he tightened his blue woolen cape around his shoulders and gave the sled a gentle tug.

Before he could take more than a few steps, a black rabbit hopped across his path. It paused to sniff the air, its whiskers trembling.

"Hey, little fella!" called Will. His voice sounded strange and hollow.

When was the last time he had spoken to someone?

Will usually traveled with his friend Mina. But this time, they had agreed to split up. He had set out north to the taiga. And she had said something about going south, toward the desert. *That's okay*, thought Will. *I'll have my own adventure.* But he had to admit, he'd gotten used to having Mina by his side.

Seeing peaceful mobs like that rabbit made him feel less lonely. There was another one now! The black rabbits were easy to spot against the snow, like ink splotches on a fresh sheet of paper.

Will watched the rabbit hopping toward him—quickly, as if it were being chased. It was moving so fast!

But, wait . . . that was no rabbit. As Will watched, the ink splotch grew in size. It wasn't really hopping—it was bounding. And as it barreled across the icy landscape, Will suddenly realized what it was.

A *wolf.*

And it was heading directly for him.

Wolves don't attack people, Will reminded himself. *Not unless we attack them first.* But his racing heart wouldn't listen. He fought the urge to turn and flee, knowing he'd never outrun the animal on this slippery path.

He grabbed his bow and arrow, but the bow was stuck on something— the strap of the sled! As the wolf grew closer, Will yanked at the bow in a panic. *C'mon!* he thought, tugging harder. But it wouldn't budge.

The wolf leaped over an icy boulder as if it were no bigger than a pebble in its path. And then he was just a few feet away, snapping and snarling at Will.

This is it, thought Will, feeling a trickle of dread run down his spine. *He's going to attack!*

CHAPTER 2

As the wolf crouched low, his back flat,
Will froze—bracing for battle.

Just before the wolf sprang forward,
a gruff voice rang out across the plains.

"Winston, SIT!"

The dog whirled around toward the
voice. He cocked his head and whined.
And then, miraculously, he sat.

A round man with a rust-red beard
popped out from behind an ice pillar

and lumbered toward Will. His leather chest plate bobbed up and down as his heavy boots crunched through the ice.

Will held his breath. He'd been taught to trust no one while exploring the Overworld. But this man looked friendly enough.

"Sorry, lad," the man said. "The dog was just protecting me, so he was. Me name's Bagley." He extended a meaty hand.

"That's a dog?" said Will. "He looks like a wolf!" Except on second glance, he didn't anymore. The dog had lowered himself to his belly and was resting his chin on the ice.

"I tamed 'im," explained Bagley. "A skeleton bone was all it took. And now he's loyal to me, so it seems."

He tamed a wolf? Will's jaw dropped. He had once tamed an ocelot in the jungle. He had named the cat Shadow and brought it back to live with Seth on the farm near Little Oak. But a wolf? That was a whole different animal.

He shivered, remembering how the dog had bared his teeth just a moment ago. "But wolves aren't supposed to attack people," said Will. "Why did he come after me?"

Bagley chuckled, his ruddy cheeks flushing a deeper shade of red. "T'was my fault," he said. "I saw a speck of blue and thought ye might be a zombie. Winston sensed my fear, so he did. It's the zombie siege in Birch Grove that's got me nerves rattled."

"Zombies? In Birch Grove?" said Will. He wasn't fond of zombies, but he wasn't really afraid of them either. They were usually too slow to do much damage. But Birch Grove was awfully close to Little Oak, Will's hometown.

Bagley nodded solemnly. "They strike the town at night and burst into flames at daybreak. And those birch houses are like kindling. When zombies burn, they can set houses aflame too."

That won't happen in Little Oak, thought Will. Seth had helped build the houses there. And they were as sturdy as could be.

But Bagley didn't seem so sure. "I'm traveling to meet me friend in the hills," he said, "to see how far this siege has spread. I'll be back in the morning. So perhaps our paths will cross again in the taiga, lad."

With another shake of Will's hand, Bagley set off across the plains. And Will pushed forward toward his adventure in the snowy taiga.

It's already been an adventure, he thought. *So far, I was mistaken for a zombie and met a wolf named Winston!*

As he glanced over his shoulder at the dog, he decided to add a third item to his taiga to-do list:

1. Throw snowballs.
2. Build a snow golem.
3. Tame a wolf.

At the top of the hill, Will sucked in his breath, taking in the winter wonderland.

White icing lined every tree branch. Blue-gray grass circled the trunks below. Bright red poppies and brown mushrooms poked through the carpet of snow. And fresh flakes fell like confetti, as if to say, "Welcome, Will. Welcome to the taiga!"

Curiosity led him higher to a cluster of moss-covered rocks. If he climbed them, he might be able to see down both sides of the mountain.

Sure enough, from his slippery stoop, he could see the ice plains stretching toward the horizon.

And down the opposite side of the mountain, he spotted a pond. A fishing pond? Or was it frozen over? He craned his neck, looking for movement on the surface of the water.

But the only movement came from the slippery rocks beneath his feet. As his foot slid sideways, he teetered. He wobbled one way, then

the other, and finally fell forward—
catching his knees on the edge of the
sled. Ouch!

The sled began to inch forward as if
in slow motion.

Will lunged to grab the strap—just
in time. One finger hooked the loop,
and he hung on tight, sprawled on his
belly across the snow.

But the sudden stop knocked the
pumpkin off its base of blankets.
It rolled like a basketball down the
sled. And with two quick bounces, it
disappeared from sight.

CHAPTER 3

"No!" Will roared as he leaped to his feet. He let go of the sled, and realized his mistake as it zoomed down the hill.

Will raced after it, following the pumpkin-turned-snowball as it bounced toward the lake. Then suddenly he was tumbling, too, gathering speed as he rolled down the hillside.

Sky. Snow. Sky. Snow. Sky. Snow.

He closed his eyes and braced for impact. Would it be water or ice? He wasn't sure—he didn't even know what to hope for.

As the ground began to level off, Will heard a distant *crack*. He slid sideways onto the ice and gradually came to a stop, staring up at the blue sky.

He lay still for a moment, until frigid water began to seep through his clothes. Then he remembered.

The pumpkin!

He shot straight up, searching. It wasn't hard to spot the orange gourd on the surface of the frozen pond. And Will instantly saw the jagged crack in its side.

He walked across the ice, slipping every few steps, and sank to his knees. One side of the pumpkin was ruined— and so were Will's dreams of making a snow golem.

And after I dragged that heavy pumpkin all the way here! he wanted to scream. He wanted to stomp on the pumpkin, crush it to a gooey pulp. But he didn't. Because the cracked gourd reminded him of something—a Jack o' Lantern.

Mina had told him once that she'd seen a snow golem made with a Jack o' Lantern head. So maybe there was hope for this pumpkin yet.

He lugged the pumpkin toward the sled, which had come to a halt at the edge of the pond.

And that's when Will saw the dark, gaping hole at the base of the hill ahead. It was a cave. *A shelter!* he realized.

He hurried toward the opening, hoping he'd find food, heat, and supplies inside. That would make his first night here in the taiga much easier.

Sure enough, a furnace sat in the middle of the crude shelter. Will held his palm a few inches above the stone oven, hoping for warmth. It was ice cold, but a bucket on the floor held lumps of coal.

Next to the bucket, Will found a sack of potatoes. Just beyond that, in a cozy corner of the cave, lay a fleece dog bed. A red collar hung from a nail above the bed, and an empty water bowl rested beside it. *Is this Bagley's shelter?* Will wondered. *Did Winston sleep here last night?*

He felt a tingle of excitement, thinking about taming his own wolf.

He'd made it to the taiga, where anything seemed possible! But he would need a skeleton bone first. And that would mean battling one of the rattling monsters.

Dusk would fall quickly here in the north—Seth had warned Will about that. So he quickly prepped the shelter for nightfall. *Bagley won't mind if I camp out here*, he decided. And when Bagley returned in the morning, he'd say that everything was all right in Little Oak—Will was sure of it.

He lit the furnace, which cast a rosy glow on the walls of the cave. Then he slid the heavy wooden door to the cave closed to keep curious mobs outside.

Next, he set to work making that Jack o' Lantern, cutting off the top and scooping out the slimy seeds and pulp.

It took half an hour before the pumpkin was hollow. As he held it up to the light, he realized something. The pumpkin was big enough to fit on his head! If he wore it like a helmet, he could actually look at an Enderman without being attacked. That would be something!

He gently lowered the pumpkin over his head, and was relieved when it actually fit. He could see through the eyeholes and breath through the jagged mouth of the Jack o' Lantern.

Night had fallen. *It's time!* he thought eagerly. Time to battle a few skeletons for bones—and maybe fight an Enderman, too!

As he slid open the heavy door, a chilly blast of night air took his breath away. He couldn't exactly see the world around him—not unless he turned his whole pumpkin-clad head, which was awkward. So instead of going in search of skeletons and Endermen, he leaned against the outer wall of the cave and waited.

Zombies moaned in the distance, but Will ignored them—he had bigger plans. He watched, waited . . . and waited some more.

Sure, thought Will. *The one time I'm ready for an Enderman, they're nowhere to be found!*

Then he heard the *thwang* of a bow.

Something struck his pumpkin head—so hard that it sent him reeling backward.

He hadn't found the skeletons. *But they found me*, he thought, sinking to his knees.

CHAPTER 4

Will scrambled backward toward
the door of the shelter. It took all his
strength to heave it open and crawl
inside. Then he reached up and tugged
at the pumpkin on his head. When it
finally came loose, he
examined it—and
nearly dropped it
in horror.

The skeleton's arrow had hit the pumpkin just millimeters above one eyehole. Will patted his forehead, feeling for blood. His skin was clammy with sweat, but he couldn't feel an open wound.

As he blew out a breath of relief, he inspected the inside of the pumpkin. Only the very tip of the arrow had pushed through the pumpkin shell. If it had gone any further, he might have been wearing that pumpkin helmet permanently.

Will paced the floor, trying to make a plan. The skeletons were still out there somewhere. And if he wanted to tame a wolf, he needed a bone—from one of those skeletons.

So he took a deep breath of courage and reached for his bow and arrow. Then he stepped back outside.

The first arrow whizzed past just inches in front of his face. But now that he wasn't wearing a pumpkin, Will dodged it easily. He ducked behind a boulder and released his own arrow. It hit bone—he could tell by the way the skeleton jumped backward.

Now's my chance, thought Will. He raced toward the skeleton, zigzagging left and right to avoid getting hit.

He launched another arrow, and then another. *Thwang! Thwack!*

The arrows hit their mark. But he'd have to get closer to finish the job.

He slid his sword from its sheath, sprinted toward the mob, and struck with all his strength.

With a rattle and a sigh, the skeleton toppled. Bones tinkled like icicles onto the ground—not just one bone, but two.

Yes!

As he stooped to collect his prize, Will heard a chorus of grunts and groans. That could mean only one thing: zombies.

Sure enough, the mob of green monsters was milling around in front of his cave. As he stood up, they staggered toward him, arms outstretched.

"You want a piece of me, slowpokes?" cried Will. After defeating the skeletons, he felt bold and ready for battle. *Maybe Bagley is afraid of zombies, but I'm not.* He raised his bow and arrow and dropped the first zombie in three seconds flat.

As the other groaning mobs approached, he reloaded—and took out two more. When he was fresh out of arrows, he grabbed his sword and sprinted forward.

Then he saw it out of the corner of his eye—four more zombies staggering out of the darkness! He slid to a stop in the snow, breathing hard. Now what? Should he fight them off or run for cover?

His body still ached from his tumble down the hill, and he couldn't catch his breath. *But zombies are easy*, he reminded himself. *Right?*

He decided to fight.

With a renewed burst of energy, he scrambled onto a rock and waited. When a dead-eyed zombie was just a couple of feet away, he leaped toward it, swinging his sword. He struck once, twice—until the zombie grunted and toppled to the snow.

The next two were tougher. Will's limbs felt heavy and cold. He had to strike several times to take down the snarling mobs. And there was still one more!

He used his last ounce of energy to lunge at the creature. But his sword barely grazed its dead green skin, and the zombie kept coming. As Will struggled to attack again, he felt like a zombie—slow and awkward.

Finally, he reduced the last zombie to a pile of steaming flesh. Then Will dropped to the ground, too—weak and tired.

Get to the shelter, he reminded himself. *Before the next mob shows up.*

But as he pushed himself up, a low growl stopped him. He turned slowly, his chest tight with fear, and came face to face with . . .

a wolf.

A very *hungry* wolf.

CHAPTER 5

The wolf wanted that rotten meat, and
she seemed to think Will did, too. As
he took a slow step backward, the wolf
stepped forward, baring her teeth.
She won't hurt me, Will told himself. But
he couldn't be sure. He tightened his grip
on his sword.

As the wolf lunged, Will pulled his
arm back, ready to strike. But something
stopped him. There was hunger in that

wolf's eyes, but there was something else, too—something familiar.

She looks like a dog, thought Will suddenly. *This wolf is just a dog, like Winston!*

He lowered his arm, hoping he was making the right decision. At the same time, he raised his other hand and dropped one of the skeleton bones. It clattered to the ground inches from his feet.

The wolf's eyes tracked the bone. She sniffed the air and cast a wary look at Will.

She licked her lips and whined, and then inched forward toward the bone.

As the wolf began to greedily lick and nibble at the treat, a slow smile spread across Will's face. *Forget Winston*, he thought. *He belongs to Bagley. But this dog is mine.*

Will woke to the chill of morning. Staring at the shadowy ceiling of the cave, he wondered aloud: "Was it a dream?"

His answer came in the form of a whine and a tail thump. The wolf—er, dog—was still here.

"Hey, girl. Hey, buddy!" Will crouched in front of the fleece dog bed and slowly extended his hand. "Should I call you Buddy?"

She sniffed Will's hand and gave a gentle lick. Then she stood up, stretched her legs, and let out a very not-wolf-like yawn.

Will laughed. "Wake up, sleepyhead, he said. "We've got lots to do today. Want to go outside?" With his new friend by his side, he couldn't wait to get out into the snow.

Buddy wagged her tail and trotted toward the door. As Will pulled it open, fresh snow fell into the shelter. He scooped some up, thrilled to feel it pack in his hands. "Perfect for snowballs, Buddy. Let's go!"

She bounded into the snow, crouching low and challenging Will to chase her. He did, tossing snowballs into the air—which Buddy jumped up and caught in her mouth.

"Yes!" said Will, pumping his fist. "Nice catch!" He laughed and scooped up more snow, playing with the dog until they were both panting loudly.

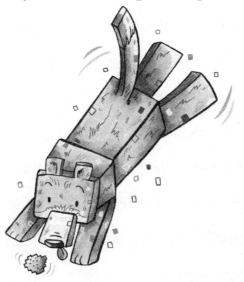

As Will plopped onto the ground for a break, Buddy trod down a bed of snow right next to him. Sitting beside his friend, Will gazed up at the sun and smiled.

"What a perfect day," he said, throwing his arm around the dog. "Nothing could make this day better." Then he remembered his to-do list. "Nothing, except maybe a snow golem. Should we get started, Buddy?"

Her tail thumped out a "yes" in the snow.

As Will looked around for the perfect patch of snow, a shadow fell over him. Something was blocking the sun. But what?

He whirled around.

Two dark figures stood on top of the hill. What were they? He squinted.

Spider jockeys!

Will sprang to his feet.

Why had they spawned in daylight?
There was no time to figure it out.
Those spider-riding skeletons were
fast and fierce. They'd be down here
in a heartbeat!

Buddy let out a low growl. She
jumped in front of Will, her body
tensed and ready for battle.

She's protecting me! Will realized.
But the last thing he wanted to do was
put his dog in danger.

"No, Buddy!" he said. "There's
two of them and one of you. You sit.
Stay." He pointed until the dog slowly
lowered her back end to the ground.
She whined, but she listened.

When Will turned back toward the spider jockeys, they were heading downhill, getting closer by the second. Close enough to strike? He raised his bow and arrow, aiming at the bobbing figure riding in the lead.

But as he squinted into the sun, he blinked. Were his eyes playing tricks on him? That skeleton was riding a horse, not a spider. And she wore her hair in a ponytail. A red ponytail.

Mina!

CHAPTER 6

"You thought I was a *what*?" cried Mina. Her voice rang out across the valley, spooking both horses—the one she was riding and the one she was leading. "You know spider jockeys only spawn at night."

Will laughed nervously. "I know. Sorry. But what are you doing here? I thought you were going to the desert!"

Mina's forehead creased with worry. "Seth sent me. There's a zombie siege in Birch Grove. Seth thinks Little Oak is in trouble, too. He needs our help."

Will sighed. "I already know about the zombie siege. But Seth can handle that, can't he? Last night, I fought off a pack of zombies all by myself." He didn't mention that it had actually been a tough battle.

Mina shook her head. "You don't get it, Will. Some of the villagers in Birch Grove were attacked. They turned into zombie villagers. Houses are already burning, and the whole town might go up in flames. Seth thinks zombies will hit Little Oak next. We can't let that happen!"

Zombie villagers? Will had heard a rumor about them, but he'd never believed it was true. "Will the zombie villagers die?" he asked.

Mina patted the saddlebags strapped to her horse. "I have the antidotes—splash potion of weakness and golden apples. But I only had enough gold to craft a few. And they'll only work if we can get to the villagers in time. We have to go to Little Oak. Now!"

Buddy whined at Will's feet. He scratched her head, trying to calm her.

"I—I can't go," he said to Mina. "I tamed a wolf, and we have all kinds of plans. We're going to make a snow golem!"

Mina furrowed her brow. "A snow golem, Will? Really? But Seth is your brother. He needs you!"

She made it sound as if making a snow golem was no big deal. *But I've waited so long to come to the taiga!* Will wanted to shout. *What if I never get the chance again?*

He said nothing. He could tell by the look on Mina's face that she wouldn't understand.

They stared at each other in frozen silence. Finally, Mina huffed, sending a puff of white mist into the air. "I guess I can't make you come with me. But I'll leave the horse for you. I really hope you change your mind, Will."

She handed him the lead rope for the second horse, a chestnut mare.

Will stared at the rope in his hand. Was he making a mistake? He couldn't tell. He only knew he couldn't say goodbye to the taiga. Not yet. He just couldn't.

Will packed together a tight ball
of snow. Then he rolled it until the
ball was as tall as Buddy. The dog
jumped backward, challenging the
snowball to a fight.

Will made a second snowball,
grunting as he lifted it onto the
first. Then he brushed the snow
off his hands and stared at the
snowman. "With coal buttons and
stick arms, you'll be a handsome
fella."

The horse whinnied from where
Will had tied her near the shelter.

"I know, I know," he said. "I shouldn't use Bagley's coal without asking. But where is he? Why isn't he back yet?"

Will glanced uphill, hoping to see Bagley lumbering down. Would he bring good news or bad about the zombie seige? Will hoped it would be good!

That would prove he had made the right decision to stay in the taiga. Then he could have some fun instead of worrying about Little Oak.

Will searched for spruce twigs on the ground, but there were none. "C'mon, Buddy," he said. "Let's look for some at the top of the hill."

Buddy happily trotted beside him. But halfway up, she took off like a shot.

"Where are you going?" Will cried. They raced to the crest, with Buddy in the lead. Then she crouched, growling.

Will spotted it, too.

A wolf was headed toward them.

Will froze, wishing he had a bone to offer. Would the wolf attack?

As soon as the animal saw them, Will had his answer. It broke into a trot, its tail wagging.

"Winston!" Will cried, rushing to meet the dog. "Where's Bagley?"

Winston barked. He ran toward the ice plains and back again, as if to say, "Follow me! Hurry!"

A pit of dread formed in Will's stomach. "Did something happen to Bagley?"

The dog answered with a pitiful whine.

Will jogged to the edge of the mountain. As he looked down over the ice plains, he saw no sign of Bagley. But something else

caught his eye—a pillar of smoke on
the horizon.

Fire! A very big fire.

It was coming from the direction of
Birch Grove—and Little Oak!

CHAPTER 7

Will half-ran, half-slid down the hill toward the shelter. He had to get to Little Oak—before the whole town burned to the ground!

Buddy and Winston raced beside him, barking madly. But by the time they reached bottom, Will had a new worry. *If Seth and a whole town of villagers can't fight off the zombies, what can I do? I'm only one boy!*

As Will leaned forward to catch his breath, Buddy licked his face. She seemed to be saying, "You've got me."

Then Winston nudged his nose under Will's arm.

Will smiled. "You're right—I'm not alone. I have the two of you. But I'd need a whole pack of wolves to fight off those zombies."

As soon as the words were out of his mouth, Will jolted upright.

"That's it!" he cried. "It's the only way to save Little Oak. But . . . we have to wait till night falls. And we're sure going to need a lot of bones."

Will was waiting in the darkness
when he heard the first rattle of
skeletons.

Buddy growled and perked up her
ears. Will searched for the bony mob,
too, but saw nothing—nothing but
the shadows of spruce trees.

As he aimed his bow and arrow into
the darkness, both dogs tensed up.
Winston paced and whined.

When an arrow whizzed by Will's
head, he ducked and released an arrow
of his own. *Thwang!*

The dogs sprang into action, tearing
through the snow toward the trees.

He raced after them, until he heard the low groan of a mob behind him. Zombies. If he killed them, they'd drop rotten flesh. And maybe that rotten flesh would lure some wild wolves.

Please let Buddy and Winston be okay, he thought, taking one last look at the forest. Then he turned around to fight.

With every swing of his sword, Will thought of Little Oak. He battled those zombies as if they were the very mobs that had set his hometown on fire.

"This one is for SETH!" he cried, striking the first mob with a wild swing.

"This is for Mina!" he said, battling the second until it dropped with a groan.

"And this is for Bagley!" he shouted, because he was pretty sure Bagley had met up with some zombies, too.

By the time the fight was over, Will's heart pounded with fury. Steam rose from the piles of rotten flesh surrounding him. He only hoped it would be enough.

Then he heard a whine from the woods. Buddy! Will raced toward the trees, slipping and tripping in the snow. He saw branches snap, and then a furry beast barreled out toward him.

"Buddy!"

She had something in her mouth. It was a glistening white bone, from a skeleton Will wouldn't have to fight because his loyal dog had killed it for him.

Will buried his face in Buddy's soft gray fur. "You're a good friend," he whispered. "The best friend ever."

Something nudged Will's arm— something cold and wet. It was Winston, who whined and dropped another bone in the snow.

"You too, Winston," said Will, scratching his ears. "I didn't mean to forget you."

As an arrow struck the spruce tree overhead, Will jumped back up. There was more work to be done. But he felt stronger, now, with his dogs by his side.

Will slipped forward in the saddle. He was half-afraid he'd slide right over the horse's head. The trail down the mountain was so steep!

But the mare was sure-footed, and if he gave her enough rope, she seemed to know what to do.

He glanced over his shoulder. There were Buddy and Winston, right on the horse's heels. And behind them? An entire pack of wolves, their loyal eyes trained on Will.

He tightened his grip on the reins. Soon, he and his pack were racing across the ice plains, the frigid wind whipping against his face. Now that Will had decided to return to Little Oak, he couldn't get there fast enough.

CHAPTER 8

The sky was dark as coal by the time
Will and his loyal wolves reached
Seth's farm.

Or what was left of it.

The black obsidian house stood
strong and tall against the night
sky, but the land around it had been
destroyed. The lush garden was
little more than a scorched fire pit,
and nearby, burnt animal pens had

toppled like twigs. A few pigs and chickens roamed freely on the hillside overlooking Little Oak.

But when Will saw the village below, he felt a wave of relief. Little Oak hadn't burned—not yet. The fire he'd seen in the distance must have been Birch Grove. So there was still time to save his village.

Meow!

The pitiful sound came from above Will's head. "Shadow!" he cried.

Was the cat in a tree? No, there he was—perched on the stone gate just out of reach. When he saw the wolves, Shadow's back arched and he let out a low *hiss*.

"It's okay," Will said soothingly. "They're here to help. We'll be back, Shadow. We're going to get Seth."

With that declaration, Will turned his horse downhill and raced toward the village, his army of wolves trailing behind.

From a distance, Little Oak looked peaceful. Gravel roads stretched out from the well at the center of the village like the spokes of a wheel. The flower and vegetable gardens looked lush and healthy, not burnt black. And the bushes surrounding each building were just as green and vibrant.

But as Will grew closer, those bushes took on new shape. They were moving. They were moaning. They weren't bushes at all.

Zombies surrounded each and every home. The writhing green masses bumped against doors and climbed over one another, trying to get through windows.

As Will galloped past the first house, he caught a glimpse of the villagers inside. One of them was a child—a terrified child. And as Will locked eyes with the boy, he knew he had to do something.

He dropped his horse's reins and drew his bow and arrow, striking a zombie in the shoulder. As soon as Will released that arrow, his wolves attacked the zombies, too.

They lunged, their jaws snapping at everything green in their path. Zombies groaned and dropped, leaving piles of rotten flesh.

Will slid off his horse and raced through town, hoping to see another human being—Mina, Seth, anyone. But all he saw was a sea of zombies.

A small cluster of them banged against the outer door of the town jail. It was an iron door, and it would never give, but it didn't seem to

matter to the zombies. Again and
again, they struck the door, scraping
at it with their fingernails.

Will couldn't stand the sight or the
sound. He raced at the zombies, sword
drawn. But something caught his
eye: their torn clothing, brown and
white. These monsters weren't wearing

tattered
blue pants,
like most
zombies.
They were
wearing
robes, robes
like . . .
    villagers.

Buddy raced past Will in a gray blur, barreling toward the zombies with her teeth bared.

For a moment, Will couldn't move—couldn't speak. Finally, he opened his mouth and forced the words out.

"No! Buddy, STOP!"

CHAPTER 9

Buddy obediently stopped—just short of
the zombie villagers. Then the front door
of the jail swung open, and Mina's red
head poked through. "Will, come on!"
she called, waving her arm. She
disappeared back
inside, but the
zombies spilled
into the jail
after her.

"Mina!" Will rushed forward. How could he get to her with the zombies in his path?

Not zombies, he reminded himself. *Zombie villagers.* That meant he couldn't kill them. He had to try to save them. But how?

Then he remembered that Mina had the potion—the one that might be able to heal them. He just hoped she could use it in time.

After the zombie villagers crossed the threshold, Will did, too. He saw with relief that Mina was luring the zombie villagers into a cell. As the last one staggered inside, she ducked and

darted out, slamming the heavy door
behind her.

"Hurry! Help me!" she called to
Will. She handed him a glass vial
filled with purple liquid. "Splash
potion of weakness. Get as much on
them as you can."

She unscrewed her own vial and splashed it through the bars of the jail cell, hitting one of the zombie villagers square in the face. The zombie hissed and stepped backward.

Will rushed toward the bars and took aim at another zombie villager— this one wearing the tattered brown robes of a farmer. He flung the liquid at the zombie again and again until rivers of purple potion trickled down its face. The monster hissed and shuddered.

Mina was emptying another bottle on the last zombie villager when she suddenly shrieked and leaped backward. "I got some on myself," she

said, wiping her arm on her T-shirt.
"Hurry, hand me that bottle." She
gestured toward a vial of red liquid
on a desk near the front door. But
before Will could get it to her, she had
slumped to the floor.

"Mina!"
he cried.
"What do
I do?"

"Throw
it," she
whispered
hoarsely.
"Throw it
at me."

He quickly unscrewed the cap and poured the red liquid over Mina. She shivered and closed her eyes tight. But when she opened them again, they were clear and bright.

"Are you okay?" he asked, squatting beside her.

"I . . . I think so," she said, scooting up and leaning against the stone wall. "Splash potion of healing—it works every time."

Splash potion of healing helps humans. But splash potion of weakness helps zombie villagers? Will shook his head. He'd never be able to keep it straight the way Mina did. She was a master brewer.

"It's really good to see you, Mina," he said, sitting beside his friend. Then he heard sounds from the other side of the iron door—the grunt of a zombie and the growl of a wolf. Buddy?

"I have to go back out," he said quickly. "Buddy might need me."

Mina grabbed his arm. "Will," she said, "there's something in here you should see first." Her icy tone surprised him, like a splash potion tossed in his face. She had bad news—he could feel it.

Mina gestured past the jail cell filled with zombie villagers, who were clustered in the corner of the cell. She pointed to the far end of the jail, where another cell sat dark and empty.

But when Will looked again, he saw that it wasn't empty. A creature stood in the shadows. What was it? Another zombie villager?

He forced himself to walk slowly toward the cell.

As he got closer, he could see the zombie villager more clearly. Torn brown overalls and a tattered plaid shirt. Dark hair, and wild eyes. The zombie villager was staring right back at him, hissing softly.

Will shivered and took another step forward. Those wild eyes looked familiar somehow, the way Buddy's eyes had during that fateful moment outside the cave in the taiga. Will squinted to see behind the monster's "mask"—to look deeper.

It took just an instant.

He recognized the creature, and the shock of it sent Will scrambling backward.

This was no zombie.

And it wasn't just another zombie villager.

The wild, miserable monster staring back at Will was his brother.

Seth!

CHAPTER 10

Will fell to the floor, pushing himself
backward away from the cell. He closed
his eyes and shook his head, trying to
wake up from the nightmare.

A hand on his shoulder startled him, and he jumped to his feet and whirled around.

"It's okay," said Mina soothingly. She was standing between him and the door.

He pushed past her, reaching for the handle. "I gotta go," he mumbled. *But where?* he wondered. *Home? Back to Seth's farm? Seth's not there! Seth's not even . . . human anymore!*

"It's not okay," he said weakly, resting his forehead against the cool iron door. "I let him down. I should have come home sooner, when he needed me."

"He'll survive," Mina said. "I think so, anyway. I gave him the splash potion. Maybe you can give him this." She reached into her sack and handed Will a golden apple. "He needs it to heal. I have some for the others, too."

Will took the heavy fruit in his palm. Then he took a deep breath and crept slowly back toward the cell.

"Don't get too close!" Mina warned. "He's still a zombie—and he's very strong."

Will paused. *He wouldn't attack me though, would he?* The thought hurt his heart. But he knew this wasn't really his brother—at least, not yet.

As Will set the apple down just inside the bars of the cell, Seth watched his every move. Then he staggered toward the apple, hissing and twitching.

"Is he in pain?" Will asked.

"He's healing," Mina reminded him. "It just takes time."

After eating the apple, Seth's twitching stopped. He took deep breaths. He even seemed to take a nap, a long nap that worried Will. But he could see his brother's chest heaving up and down, so he knew that Seth was still living—still fighting.

When he finally woke up, he looked more like Seth. His skin color had shifted from green back to golden brown. His eyes seemed more friendly, and when he looked at Will, he actually seemed to see him.

As a sliver of morning light slid beneath the door of the jail, Seth spoke. "Will?"

"Yes!" cried Will, leaping up. "Are you okay? How do you feel?" He rattled the bars of the jail cell, eager to get inside with Seth.

Mina fumbled to find the key on the ring, finally pushing the right one through the keyhole and swinging the door open.

Will rushed into the cell to hug his brother. Seth felt hot and sweaty, as if he'd been fighting a high fever. But he was himself. He was human. And he was alive.

Will heard the jangle of keys as Mina released the other zombie villagers—including the town librarian, who seemed dazed as she examined her tattered white robe. "Is it morning?" she asked.

Mina nodded. But Will caught the alarm in her voice when she said, "I'm afraid it is."

"That means the zombies are gone," said Will. "Little Oak is safe now, right?"

Mina corrected him. "It means the zombies burned. But the town may be burning, too." She pointed toward a thin plume of smoke rising from beneath the jailhouse door. Then she shot Will a determined look and said, "We have to go. Now."

CHAPTER 11

As Mina flung open the jailhouse door, smoke billowed in. Will pushed through it, leading Seth by the hand.

"Buddy? Winston?" Will called out. But as smoke filled his lungs, he started to cough.

Small fires burned everywhere. The zombies were gone, but they'd left mass destruction: burning doors, bushes, and houses.

Will suddenly remembered the faces he'd seen through the window of one of those houses. Were villagers still trapped inside?

"We need water!" he hollered, rushing toward the cobblestone well. He cranked the lever, raising a bucket full of ice-cold water, and handed it to Mina. He brought up bucket after

bucket, until his shoulders ached. Seth helped carry the water, and so did other villagers as, one by one, they were rescued from their burning homes.

"I'll take over now, lad," someone said from over Will's shoulder. Bagley!

"You're okay!" Will shouted, giving the burly man a hug. "I thought . . ."

"You thought the zombies did me in, did you?" asked Bagley. "When I saw what they did to Birch Grove, I came to Little Oak to help. Turns out you helped me, now didn't you? I was trapped inside with the villagers. Lost me dog in Birch Grove, too." His face darkened.

"No, Winston is here!" Will cried. "He came to tell me about you. He's here—somewhere." Will hoped his words were still true, that Winston would show up unharmed.

Tears welled in Bagley's eyes. "Thank you, lad," he said. "That does me heart good. Now, let's put out this fire."

He cranked the lever furiously, bringing up another bucket.

Someone else wanted to help, too. As Will handed off a bucket of water, something nudged his leg. Buddy looked up as if to say, "What can I do?"

Will dropped and buried his face in Buddy's fur. "I'm so glad you're okay, girl," he whispered.

She was right there, as always. But there was nothing more she could do for him—no more monsters to fight. Just a town to put back together.

"Just sit, Buddy," Will said with a smile. "Stay." But he already knew that she would.

"Will it ever be the same?" asked Will as he and Seth walked through what was left of Little Oak. The houses were charred, wet, and smoking.

"It won't be the same," said Seth. He took a deep breath and squared his shoulders. "But it might be even better. We'll replace the wooden doors with iron ones, and we'll raise the entrances a foot or two—to keep the zombies out." His eyes brightened at the thought.

Will could tell Seth was already getting excited about the building project. He laughed and shook his head. His brother was back!

"Watch yer step, lad," shouted Bagley from behind.

Will glanced down and narrowly missed stepping into a pile of rotten zombie flesh. It was everywhere. Here and there, a stray wolf feasted—Will's wolves, who had been loyal and fought off those zombies to the bitter, burning end.

Beside him, Buddy looked tired, her tail hanging low. Winston did, too, as he padded along after Bagley. *But at least we're all okay*, thought Will. *And we're together*.

As they walked on, he noticed that zombies had dropped other things besides rotten flesh—carrots, potatoes, and even a few iron bars. He reached down to pick one up. The iron felt solid and heavy in his hand. It gave him an idea.

"I know another way to protect Little Oak," he said, standing back up. "We can build a golem—an iron golem!"

He quickly told Seth about the snow
golem he had wanted to build in the
taiga. "I never got to do it—I came
home first. But that's okay, because
an iron golem is so much better. And
bigger. And tougher. Those dirty
zombies wouldn't stand a chance!"

Seth slowly smiled. "That's a great idea," he said. "Maybe I can help you build it." Then he turned to face his brother. "Thanks, Will."

"For what?"

"For coming back. For helping me and Little Oak. We really needed you."

Will's cheeks warmed with pride—and embarrassment. He shrugged and said, "That's what we do, right? We stick together, no matter what."

Buddy was still at his feet, never far away. That dog was the best friend a boy could hope for. But Seth? *He's my brother*, Will reminded himself. *And I'll never let him down again.*